TRAPPED IN HEAVEN AND OTHER STORIES

9 STORIES ON LOVE & RELATIONSHIPS

MAYURA AMARKANT

Copyright © Mayura Amarkant
All Rights Reserved.

ISBN 978-1-63873-958-6

This book has been published with all efforts taken to make the material error-free after the consent of the author. However, the author and the publisher do not assume and hereby disclaim any liability to any party for any loss, damage, or disruption caused by errors or omissions, whether such errors or omissions result from negligence, accident, or any other cause.

While every effort has been made to avoid any mistake or omission, this publication is being sold on the condition and understanding that neither the author nor the publishers or printers would be liable in any manner to any person by reason of any mistake or omission in this publication or for any action taken or omitted to be taken or advice rendered or accepted on the basis of this work. For any defect in printing or binding the publishers will be liable only to replace the defective copy by another copy of this work then available.

Dedicated to those who remain trapped in their own heavens. You know who you are!

Contents

Disclaimer — vii

Acknowledgements — ix

Foreword — xi

1. Trapped In Heaven — 1
2. Sealed With A Kiss — 6
3. Be Mine — 10
4. Don't Bother Me. I'm Living Happily Ever After — 16
5. #nofilter — 23
6. Locked In A Closet With A Stranger — 27
7. Bullet In The Heart — 31
8. The Devil's Bride — 36
9. A God Named Sin — 40

Author Bio — 45

Disclaimer

Copyright @ 2020 Sarvashreshtha Solutions LLP and Mayura Amarkant. All rights reserved.

This book is a work of fiction. Names, characters, businesses, organizations either are the product of the author's imagination or are used fictitiously. Any resemblance to actual persons, living or dead, events, or locales is entirely coincidental.

This book or parts thereof may not be reproduced or sold in any form, stored in any retrieval system, or transmitted in any form by any means – electronic, mechanical, photocopy, recording, or otherwise – without prior written permission of the publisher.

Published by Sansi Ventures, the publishing arm of Sarvashreshtha Solutions LLP, Mumbai through Notion Press.

Disclaimer:The Hindi songs used in the stories don't belong to the author or the publisher. The author has used them in a colloquial manner to take the narrative forward. All the original copyrights of the songs remain with the respective creators.

Acknowledgements

Sometimes we forget to thank those who are closest to our hearts. I am therefore starting this page by thanking my biggest critics and supporters - my son, Abhimanyu and my husband, Amarkant Jain.

This book wouldn't have been possible without the encouragement and support of my in-laws, Krishankant & Saroj Jain. My co-sisters, Sushma & Amita and co-brothers, Jitendra & Aalok deserve a special mention for their unconditional love and constant faith in my abilities.

Heartfelt gratitude to team Blogchatter, Richa Singh and Vikas Agarwal for their faith.

Thank you, Niranjan Ranade, for the fascinating cover page design.

I dedicate this book to my daughter, Sanskriti, who believes that her mother is an awesome writer. Her faith propels me to write better–every time.

And finally, I thank you, dear readers, for investing your time in reading this book.

Foreword

Hi readers. I am Amarkant Jain aka Happy. Happy is happy to write this foreword for Mayura Amarkant aka Happiness, my soulmate, for her collection of short stories named 'Trapped in Heaven and other stories'.

It has been over 2 decades now that I know Mayura and one thing that I can vouch for and guarantee you about her writing is that, once you pick up any book of hers', you won't put it down till the time you finish reading it.

Her style of writing is such that you can actually sense the writing moving like a movie in front of you. All your senses are activated. The simple formula she uses to get this effect on her readers is that she always keeps her readers in mind. Like any professional method actor, who gets under the skin of the character she or he plays, as a writer, Mayura too gets under the skin of her characters and in fact, starts believing that they are real. Once you start reading her book, you too will feel the same. Although she writes fiction, her fiction is very much believable.

Her book is like a readymade screenplay for any director or film maker, who can simply adapt the book in to a movie or a web-series for any OTT platform.

She is so contemporary yet traditional and at the same time surreal, that you will start feeling that you know this character well and have interacted with her/him at some point of time in your life.

All 9 stories in this book are based on the theme of LOVE, be it with a person, thing, or their belief system.

The stories will take you down memory lane and tickle you with the emotions that you might have buried for a while.

My personal favourite is #NoFilter and I am certain that you too will have a favourite one once you read the book.

Mayura is a completely different person in real life than what you might think of her, when you read her book. She is an abundance of positive energy and life of the people around her. I always address her as Happiness. She owns a magnetic personality and is extremely passionate about her writing.

I always wish her the best she deserves and I strongly believe that her time has come and she has arrived as regards to new-age authors, who gauge the pulse of their audience and transfer them to a place where the action is happening in the book.

Eagerly awaiting for her next release.....JHUMKI...

I

Trapped in Heaven

She was standing at her favourite spot at the veranda, engrossed in her dreams. Her slender frame & silken complexion complemented the simplicity of her desires. Every afternoon, she snatched a few moments of peace from her hectic day. The breath-taking view from her palatial mansion always mesmerised her on a drizzly day. Rain-bathed nature was a treat to watch. These were some of the perks of staying at the outskirts of the busy city of Mumbai.

27-year-old Rukmini's childlike face lit up every time a gust of wind sprayed a shower of rain towards her. Droplets of water danced with her waist-length hair. She drifted into her dream world. During this season she cherished the long bike rides with him. As he navigated through the roads, she snuggled closer. They enjoyed challenging the winds that threatened to throw the bike off-balance. Her laughter resonated in the air as she opened her arms and glanced up at the sky. The breeze played with her hair as she praised God for the overwhelming feeling of being the chosen one.

.... *ting tong.... ting tong... ting tong.... ting tong*

The incessant buzz of the doorbell shook her trail of thoughts. Her 6-year-old son was back from school. He threw his things all over the house, leaving the clutter for her to clean. She followed him around the house and chided him for the litter he had caused. She watched him in awe as he narrated his day to her. Within a few minutes, he started complaining, "Mamma, I am hungry!" She served him snacks and remained beside him. He gobbled his *poha* and gulped half a glass of milk before dashing downstairs to play.

As soon as he took off, she breathed a sigh of relief and moved back to the veranda. Today was the first rain, and the smell of the wet mud trailed right up to her home. She was lost in her daydreams and felt that the routine was being a hurdle to her pleasure.

'Pyaar hua, ikrar hua hai, pyaar sey phir kyon darta hai dil' - the air resounded with delightful melodies. Far among the rose bushes in the next bungalow stood Colonel Aunty. Rukmini waved at her, Aunty sent her blessings with a cheerful grin and continued singing.

Colonel Aunty, as people addressed her, was the wife of a commanding army officer. They adored each other and remained cocooned in eternal love. One day, her husband went on a secret mission. She refused to accept the box of crushed bones that the army issued a month later.

Since that day, she wakes up at dawn, takes an hour-long shower, wears clean clothes, spritzes perfume and waits at the porch for her husband's arrival. The garden echoes with melodies she hums in the memory of her beloved companion:

Kaho ki apni preet ka geet na badlega kabhi,
Tum bhi kaho is raah ka meet na badlega kabhi
Pyaar jo toota, saath jo chhoota, chand na chamkega kabhi

Aa ha, aa ha aaa
Pyaar hua, ikraar hua hai, pyaar se phir kyun darrta hai dil...

Days like today made romance swell up in Rukmini's heart. She felt a queer yet satisfying surge of optimism in her mundane life. She adored the long drives in the Audi Q7–his favourite car. On many cold, stormy mornings, he gave the chauffeur a day off. They escaped to the hill station nearby. He drove through the heavy rains while she spotted waterfalls through the fog. Her animated laughter reverberated through the air as Jagjit Singh's soothing voice added melody to their romance.

Tera chehara hai aaine jaisa - (2)
Kyun na dekhu hai dekhne jaisa
Tera chehara hai aaine jaisa

He mouthed the lyrics, ran his index finger over her lips and kissed her intensely. She resisted and asked him to pull over. The car stopped at the corner and they made out wildly as the raindrops & fog played with the car. As they kissed, her heart was filled with a liberated sense of being loved.

A baby's wails filled the room and once again her train of reflections broke. She rushed to the bedroom. Her 1-year-old son was searching for his mother. She affectionately scooped the little one in her arms and rocked him gently. He gurgled as his mother softly sang his favourite lullaby. While tugging at her long, lustrous hair, he hungrily suckled at his Mamma's bosom. After some time, Rukmini carried him out and plonked him on the mini swing.

She sat beside him on the floor, away from the balcony but still close to her fantasy. Her view was restricted but her thoughts travelled beyond the horizon. Nothing and no one could stop her today. The fresh scent of the wet earth created a trance-like state for the die-hard romantic inside her.

Counting beads kept her toddler busy while her flight of fantasy transported her to the promenade near the Worli Seaface. The high tide threatened to swallow anyone at the seashore. Scores of people gathered during the rains and squealed in delight when an enormous wave drenched them. The deck fascinated her at this time of the year. The whiff of hot corn filled the air.

ting tong...

The single doorbell meant that her in-laws were at the door. She dutifully greeted them. They lovingly placed their hands on her head as she bent forward to take blessings. They were very proud that despite having so many servants, Rukmini loved to serve them herself. They took pride because their daughter-in-law was always at their beck and call. The rest of the day passed like any other. She cooked sumptuous meals for everyone and lovingly tended to the family's needs. While she spread happiness among her family members, her lonely heart was crying for his companionship.

Gopi had sent Rukmini a diamond necklace and flowers in the morning to earmark their 7th wedding anniversary. His mother happily received the parcel from Gopi's assistant. Her in-laws were gloating in pride as they boasted over the phone to the relatives.

Rukmini's *Amma* spoke to her excitedly and thanked her stars that her daughter was blessed with such a loving husband. She looked down coyly, fidgeting with her dupatta. Her heartfelt warm and the feeling of impending happiness nudged her. A smile crept into her eyes as she thought to herself, "Maybe he will come early today, maybe he will be in an excellent mood. Who knows... maybe tonight... hmm?"

She picked up the shirt that her husband wore yesterday and washed off the lipstick marks. She muttered under her breath, "God knows how he gets these. Maybe the elevator was crowded." After completing her daily chores, she tucked her family to bed and ran to take a bath. She hummed her favourite song, *'Sajana hai mujhe, Sajana ke liye'* as she dressed in a wine-red satin nightdress, applied light make-up, styled her hair and donned his favourite perfume. Her eye was on the clock, and she kept checking her phone for messages and calls.

Her heart was pounding as the clock was ticking, the doorbell would ring anytime now. She knew that as soon as she answered the door, he would scoop her in his arms and kiss her passionately. She wondered impatiently, "Why wasn't it ringing?"

She remembered the romantic manner in which they brought in the anniversary last night. She hugged him tightly and kissed him on his cheeks while he was answering an important call. She noticed a red mark on his neck. Maybe a rash? She ignored it and cuddled him. She had thought to herself, "He is so busy all the time, he does not mean to ignore me... or..."

Just then the phone rang, and she happily ran to answer it. Before she could say anything his quiet voice at the other end said, "Tell Papaji and Mummyji not to wait for me. I will be late again. Good night."

Her heart sank, and she felt a dagger pierce through her core. She stepped towards the window and saw Colonel Aunty dressed in a blue silk nightdress eagerly waiting at her porch.

Both were trapped in heaven.

II

Sealed with a Kiss

"One kiss, Mythu, what harm will it do? I am eighteen years old and have never kissed a girl. My friends laugh at me in college." Satya looked at her imploringly.

Mythili threw her head back and laughed, "So approach someone else, why me?" He pulled her closer and whispered in her ears, "Because you are so beautiful and you want it as badly as me..." He paused and whispered, "You want it Mythu... don't you?"

His warm breath made her ears go red; her chest was tied into a knot. She felt her cheeks burning as she looked into his intense brown eyes. A tingling sensation passed through her nerves, she looked away and she crossed her legs.

13-year-old Mythili was sitting in the colony's park with her best friend, Satyendra. Despite their 5-year age difference, they got along since childhood. They loved playing 'House-House' where rowdy Satya played Daddy and cute Mythu played the pregnant Mummy who brought home a baby from the hospital. They put up dance performances for all key events at the colony. No one ever heard of them fighting. They were always seen together; Satya always led, and Mythu followed him everywhere like a puppy.

As they grew up, their conversations changed. They spoke about studies, crushes, the latest fads and much more. He was training to be a Chartered Accountant, and she was preparing for her 8th-grade final examinations. Every day, they met an hour earlier than the rest of the gang and gossiped. One such day, Mythu shared that she had accidentally stumbled upon a kissing scene on a web series. She confessed how that passionate lip lock made her perspire every time she thought about it. Satya had pounced on the idea like a hungry wolf and was pursuing her like crazy.

Satya had grown up to be a handsome and articulate boy who stood at about 165 cm tall. His stature did not stop him from being Mr. Popular at college. She had experienced a growth spurt just after she turned 13. Spending hours in front of the mirror admiring her new curves, soft skin and silken hair was her latest habit. Sometimes she stole her mom's phone and clicked mirror selfies only to delete them immediately. Her parents had a strict, "no-social media" policy at their home, so she satiated her curiosity by reading sex advice columns in the daily newspaper.

When she saw the kissing scene in the web series, she could not stop thinking about it. She dreamed of kissing Satya under the moon and woke up with a start, perspiring profusely. When he suggested sharing their first kiss, she played hard to get and brushed him aside.

Ever since she was a kid, she had known no other man. She cherished their conversations. They shared their deepest secrets and loved hanging out with each other.

After a few days of passionate pursuit by Satya, Mythu relented. He identified a building at the far end of the colony. The top floors were empty and no one ever went there. He smuggled a broom and a clean bed sheet and set up a cosy corner on the terrace. He cradled her hand and led her to the place.

For the first time, both of them were quiet. He hugged her and cupped her face in his hands. Her lips were quivering while her entire body was on fire. She wanted to run but was weak in the knees. "Hey, Mythu, open your eyes and look at me." She looked into his eyes. He seemed like a stranger. She had never seen lust in his eyes before. He started kissing her.

She did not understand how to do this and kept pecking at his lips. "Use your tongue." He said. "Eeks!" She thought to herself. He was struggling to get it right with her, and she stood there frozen in time. They continued kissing and then stepped away from each other.

"Let's try one more time, okay Baby?" He said. "Huh, Baby? Why would he call me that?" Mythu thought to herself. They stepped closer and started kissing again, Satya felt a bulge in his pants and tried to guide her hand downwards. She resisted. He started moving his hands up her back and brought them to the front. She moved them away. They continued pecking for some time and then gave up.

She stopped, turned, and ran down the stairs. The high-pitched clomps of her slippers resonated in the air. An old uncle came out of his home to check what the commotion was about. Satya crouched and hid as he watched Mythu running away. Countless questions haunted him as he descended and retraced his steps back home.

The following days witnessed an empty wooden bench at the park and a withdrawn Mythu walking towards the market and back. At the colony, near the park, in the elevator - just anywhere she met him - she would blush and start breathing heavily. If she knew that Satya was going to be at a particular place, she would drop in, dressed in smart casuals and smelling like a garden. Their conversations had ended.

Things got out of hand when she wrote her first love letter to him. Mythu poured her feelings on a piece of paper and nervously handed it over to Satya at the park. He opened the letter in the privacy of his room. His face turned ashen as he read and comprehended each word.

He read it again just before tearing it to shreds. He convinced his parents and scuttled to a bigger city to pursue further studies. Mythu almost fainted when she heard the news. She searched him on social media, texted him, mailed him - but to no avail. Satya never turned back.

10 years later...

She blossomed into a young and successful career woman who continued to search for him... an endless search... never yielding.

One hot October afternoon, she drifted into the past, flashes of the evening on the terrace ran through her mind's eye. Her body writhed and there was worry written all over her face. He put his arms around her. She woke up with a start, drenched in a cold sweat. Vinod had returned early and slipped into bed beside her. She cuddled closer to her husband and put her head on his chest. He held her firmly and kissed her on the forehead.

It was not the same feeling. It never will be.

III

Be Mine

The tiny one-bedroom apartment in Mumbai's humble but elite, Santa Cruz East echoed with Mohan's cheerful voice. He jumped on to the bed and sang into his hairbrush. After splashing extra cologne, he adjusted his favourite shirt and stepped out. A gut feeling told him that today was going to a fabulous day. The Bandra-Worli Sea Link had opened to the public, and he had chosen this day to confess his love to Nina. His breath turned faster as he started his car. The mobile rang, Nina's name flashed on the screen and his heart jumped into his mouth.

"Where are you, Mohan? I am waiting at the signal since the last 7 minutes!" she shrieked into the phone. Her voice was music to his ears. "Hello... hello... Mohan, am I audible? Where the hell are you?" her voice shook him out of his dream world. "Yes, yes Ninu... I mean Nina, I am on my way. Should be there in 5 minutes max!" he replied.

He tuned in to his favourite song on the car stereo as he zoomed off to pick up the treasure of his soul.

'Dil ibadat kar raha hai,
Dhadkane meri sun,

Tujhko main kar loon hasil,
Lagi hai yahi dhun'

He nodded as he hummed the last sentence. Yes, soon Nina will be his, forever. A serpentine queue of cars blocked the route, as if every car in Mumbai was riding to Bandra-Worli Sea Link. His thoughts turned to the files on the seat next to him. He picked them and placed them on the rear seat. The red file with "Sentario Brothers LLP" grabbed his attention. His mind raced to the day when he first experienced a strong chemistry with Nina.

Amidst an intense brainstorming session, Nina and Mohan had abruptly started completing each other's sentences. He stared at her through the corner of his eyes as her cleavage peeped through her low-cut blouse. His eyes met hers, and he glanced elsewhere.

The water cooler gang at work had secretly named 26-year-old Nina Saxena, 'Saxy'. They used to hide in the corridors and placed bets on the number of times her *pallu* was going to slip. She always appeared to have had a busy morning. Her translucent chiffon sari swished as she raced to her cabin. She reapplied her lipstick and tamed her waist-length hair by running her well-manicured fingers through it. Her delicate fingers pinched her bra-strap in between her boobs to adjust them. This was a perpetual habit. Her *pallu* lay carelessly thrown over her shoulder and slipped each time she crossed paths with their employer, Venkat Narayan.

During client presentations, she pleated her *pallu* across half her breast and swept her hair over her right shoulder. She was favoured among clients and had sprinted her way to the top. As chief of Marketing, a squad of 25 people reported to her. During team briefings everyone clamoured for aisle seats as it offered a fantastic side view of her bare midriff and full rack. She was an aphrodisiac that allowed men's fantasies to soar.

"Hey Mr. Sharma, a moment please?" She called out to him after the discussion. They connected and started meeting for lunch every day. They carpooled to and from work often and a wonderful friendship blossomed. Mohan was just another ordinary guy. He was a medium-built, average-looking, 29-year-old engineer who had come to Mumbai in search of a better existence. He hid his intense eyes behind rimmed glasses and kept to himself. His co-workers found him cooperative and inspirational. As the commander of the Logistics department, he ensured that he supported the revenues. His sense of humour and amiable nature made him very popular.

The loud hooting of the horn jolted him out of his reverie. WTF! Six cows sat in the middle of the highway, and they refused to move! Cars tried to go around them and caused a bigger traffic jam. Drivers pounded on their horns, still others stuck their heads out of the window and abused. Among the chaos, his phone rang again. "*Yaar Mohan, kya hua? Kidhar pahuche*? 16 minutes have passed. What's the problem?" Nina sounded desperate. "I am coming, Nina. There's a huge traffic jam on the highway. You find some shade and sit. I am reaching in approximately 10 minutes." He responded as calmly as he could.

He got out of the car and began directing the traffic. After 3-4 minutes, the street got cleared. The cows got off the highway, and vehicles started gliding. "Be mine, Ninu, Be Mine!" He kept repeating this sentence to himself and practiced his moves. He interlocked his fingers on the steering wheel and drove at a steady speed.

He pictured her in a light-yellow chiffon sari and a halter-neck blouse. The skin on her delicate shoulders glistened under the lights of the bridge. She stood at the promenade when he approached her. They came close, and he was about to kiss her when the loud cry of a horn startled him. Gosh! Mumbai city and its travel woes! Can't a man drive and daydream in peace?

... they went across the bridge and into the aisle... the priest announced them husband and wife... and said... you may now kiss the bride... he bent to kiss her...bells rang around him... *arre...yeh kya ho gaya*...the bells turned into the sound of blaring horns.... and... he was jolted back to reality... his car inched forward in the crazy Mumbai traffic. Above all the ruckus and stench of petrol & car exhaust, he detected a hint of her perfume. During the regular carpool, she sometimes bent forward to change the channel and his nose caught a whiff of the heavenly scent. The tiny baby in his arms had a unique smell though. He held the baby close and kissed its little forehead. A hand touched him on his shoulder. Nina looked tired but happy on the hospital bed. She smiled weakly and whispered, "Congratulations, Jaan!" He beamed and shifted closer to smooch her.

Honk honk.... *abey.... kya karta hai...aagey jaa*...screamed the driver from the car... WTF *yaar*! He tried to focus on his driving and continued rehearsing his lines. "Be mine, Ninu. Be mine!" He remembered how he had missed work because of a terrible bout of dengue. She called him every single day and dropped in at his tiny bachelor pad, with warm, homemade soup. They played cards, sang songs and watched a film on TV. When he walked into the office after his illness, everyone clapped. She strode to him and hugged him. He still recalled her hot breath on his ear lobes as she whispered, "Missed you".

He stopped the car at their daily meeting place. "My goodness! What took you so long?" He turned to the window, and his eyes captured a full view of her cleavage. He turned towards the road. She plonked herself on the passenger seat. Her breasts jiggled at the movement as her magical aura and mind-blowing perfume filled the car. He peered at her. His heart pumped with joy. Her animated and vulgar exterior concealed a gracious soul. Yes, she was a pure-hearted soul... his Nina.

She was gesticulating, "I have so much to tell you! Hey... hey... Mohan, are you even listening to me?" She snapped her fingers in front of his blank eyes... snap.... Snap... SNAP! "... *Arre*... Mohan... what happened? Stop staring!" It astonished him when he heard her saying, "Mohan....! I got engaged!!" She giggled. He applied brakes in a hurry, the car screeched to a halt and vehicle drivers honked and hurled abuses at him. It didn't matter anymore. She exclaimed, " Mohan! What is wrong with you"? He continued staring at her. Is this why they never kissed, in his fantasies?

He muttered, "Congratulations, Nina. Who is the lucky fellow?" "You won't believe it! It is our boss, Venkat Sir! He proposed over the weekend in the most romantic manner at the Taj Resort. I couldn't refuse." He gasped and exclaimed, "What? Nina, he is twenty-five years older than you!" She smirked, replied, "Yes, he will die early! So what? Being his bride will catapult my career! Don't you see that?" Mohan gulped and acknowledged.

They passed the Bandra-Worli Sea Link, and he thought of jumping from the bridge. She continued pouring out details on how brides in Venkat's family wore more than 100 kgs gold at the marriage. He had promised her a honeymoon in Hawaii. After their wedding, he would whisk her away to his penthouse at Malabar Hill in South Mumbai. Throughout her chatter, each of Mohan's dreams popped into nothingness.

They reached the office. She alighted, adjusted her pallu, and moved briskly towards the elevator. She halted, looked behind, and shouted. "Hey Mohan, you coming?" He grinned sheepishly and replied, "You race ahead, I won't be able to keep pace."

That evening, he drove back. Same road, same traffic, same chaos, a different Mohan.

Something inside him, died.

IV
Don't Bother Me. I'm Living Happily Ever After

"Ramchandra! Gate *kholo*...."

"Ramchandra... *Idhar aao*..."

"Ramchandra.... Ramchandra... RAMCHANDRA!!!"

He ran helter-skelter when he heard her silky voice booming through the corridors.

"*Ah...aaya...aa...ayyaa...Maa...Maedumm!*" He ran towards her with his hand on his head to save his cap from falling. He stammered when he felt nervous, much to the amusement of his friends and colleagues. He enjoyed being the butt of jokes among his friends. They filled his quiet life with sounds. Whenever they teased him, he beamed happily. He loved the attention. His ordinary face, dark complexion and uniform made him look like the thousands of security guards that stand outside every building gate. His uniform didn't hide his pot-belly; another trademark of a security guard in a gigantic city like Mumbai.

Underpaid. Ignored. Exploited. Lonely. These four heartless words summarised Ramchandra's life. He hailed from a tiny village 65 km from Indore in the heart of Madhya Pradesh. A tiny cluster of 25 huts–a nameless village, too small to have a name. Or maybe it did have a name, but Ramchandra didn't know it. The inhabitants called it the hutment near the well (*kue ke paas wale ghar*). The villagers worked as daily wage labourers who tilled the land around the village. They earned a meagre salary that allowed them to afford a square meal.

Modernisation had still not reached this part of India – there was no electricity or water connection. The village well was the only source of potable water. Letters took 15-20 days to reach and one had to walk 5 kms to make a phone call. The villagers married off their daughters early, so they had one less mouth to feed. At 7, Ramchandra got married off to 4-year-old Chandralekha. She delivered a son when she turned 13 and the entire village celebrated a male child's arrival.

5 children and 8 years later, doom struck the happy hamlet. A rich man swooped upon the village like a mighty eagle and snatched away their homes. He had papers to prove that the hutment was illegal. Rendered homeless and jobless, they wandered in the scorching May heat. His father's friend, Atmaram Choubey, offered them respite in the sweltering heat. After a few days, they got shunted to a small hut. He had an enormous family: his wife, 5 children, parents, brother, sister-in-law, and their 3 children fought for space. They built a tiny shed beside the hut, and the men slept under that.

He snuck into the hut at night and climbed on his wife. She was always exhausted and lay like a log while he pumped his manliness into her weak body. When he used to leave, he sometimes crossed paths with his brother sneaking into the hut. They exchanged an awkward smile and turn their faces in opposite directions. There was no space in the tiny hut and it was pitch dark at night. He wasn't sure but believed that he once climbed on his sister-in-law and she seemed to enjoy it. She caressed his back and moaned; her skin felt so soft. He brushed aside the thought each time it arose.

They lived in extreme poverty during those days. The women managed the home and performed odd jobs to earn money. The men worked in the fields of rich zamindars who exploited them for money. Ramchandra thanked his stars that this village was better than the earlier one. Letters took 4-5 days to reach and the nearest telephone booth was 3 km away. For 2-3 years, they lived a frugal existence, till his wife told him that the stork would visit... for the 6th time. He thought to himself, there had to be other means of survival. As he wiped the perspiration from his brow, he scratched his head to think of a solution.

The next day, while rummaging through his belongings, he found a visiting card. The tiny bowl of coins next to the little temple in his hut came to his rescue. He clutched the coins and walked briskly in the scorching heat for the next 1 hour and reached the STD booth to make a phone call. His trembling fingers dialled the number. After a few failed attempts, the call connected:

"*Sh....Sh...Shukkklaa ji...helloooo...hayluuu...Hum bol rah ahu...Ramchandar...pichle saal jaade mein Gulshanwa ke byaah mein mile the...*" He stammered, his feet trembled in fear as the voice at the other end listened and replied. Ramchandra continued,

"J...jh...jee...jee...Ramchandar...haan...jee...naukri chahiye tha...koi bhi...pa..paa..pagaar...aacchha hoona chahiye...Jee...accha...aa jaayenge...kkk...kal...kal nikalte hai..tatkal sey...aaa...aaa...teey hai...Bammmbaiii..."

He hung up before his coins ran out. His heart jumped with joy. A flicker of hope in his grim life. He had encountered the lion-hearted Shuklaji at a wedding last winter. Shiv Prakash Shukla was a sharp man who loved to speak while *paan* swam in his mouth. He bragged about Mumbai, the city of gold where an ordinary bus conductor became a superstar and a driver became an industry icon. The same place where '*Abbey Shukle ke bacche!*' became the respected 'Shuklaji'. He loved boasting about his *paan* shops and security business in Mumbai.

Ramchandra bade Chandralekha goodbye amongst the howls of his 6 kids and 4 nieces and nephews. (Just after his wife delivered, his sister-in-law got pregnant as if this were a race.) His brother hugged him, and his parents showered blessings. "*Khub paisa kamana, idhar ghar le sake, utna. Jaao beta, khub tarakki karo*" His father blessed him. The blank cheque was leaving to get encashed in Mumbai.

He landed at the crowded station in Mumbai as scared as a mouse. The aura of the busy energy engulfed him. Shuklaji met him at the station and served as a mentor to date. Each day was as mundane as the other. He didn't realise that 15 years had passed since he first came to Mumbai. For the last one and half decades, he worked in the same place as a security guard. Each day, he woke up at 5 AM in a dingy 100 sq. feet shanty shared by 13 others. Going to the bathroom was a warlike scene every morning. Ramchandra tried to wake up before the others to finish his morning routine.

Preparing breakfast for 14 people was his responsibility. After cooking, he heaped a pile of the food on his plate and gobbled it with a cup of tea. They allocated the most arduous duty on the roster to him. He had to stand outside the gate and direct the traffic. He shouted at miscreants throughout the day. His weapons were his screeching whistle and a baton. This was the best job an uneducated, unlisted man could get in Mumbai. After 12 hours of rigorous duty, he rushed home and helped with cooking and cleaning. After dinner, he crashed into his bed and dozed off immediately.

Every month, he sent a lion-share of his salary to his village. 10-12 days a month, he performed a 24-hour duty routine just to earn extra money. Feeding so many mouths was a daunting task. He missed his wife and children a lot. He just wanted Chandralekha to press his tired legs while his children recited English poems that he never understood.

Once a month he would call Chandralekha who would be waiting at the STD booth. She spoke very less. She blurted a list of demands and some routine news and then turned silent. They hung up like strangers. Having someone who wanted to speak to him was enough for him to sleep that night. When he visited his village once a year, he felt like an outsider in his own home. He was uncomfortable at the unusual closeness Chandralekha, and his brother shared. During meal times she always served him after his brother. After a few days of rest, his father inquired about his return. He expressed how the money flow needed to begin again. Ramchandra also yearned to go back to Mumbai – the city he felt one with.

His life continued this way until one day, she came into his life–his *Memsahib*. She was the most powerful lady in the building. People shivered when she walked through the corridors. On Ramchandra's lucky day, she was fretting and fuming because someone caught a security guard taking bribes. Shuklaji stood there imploring her to wait for a few days as his best guard was on holiday. She looked around and her eyes met Ramchandra's nervous gaze. She asked Shuklaji to send Ramchandra as the additional guard at her office. Shuklaji started giving her excuses, but she was adamant.

As the feeling sunk in, it overwhelmed Ramchandra so much that he wanted to cry. The cool air of the air conditioner was like heaven. The tranquillity in this office was soothing to his worn-out ears. He worked very hard to earn praises from his new *Memsahib*. He had grown fond of her grace and élan. It was rare to find a person like her. She mesmerised everyone with her manner of speaking.

She was his holy goddess. There was only one problem he did not understand how an office worked. Despite his efforts, he ended up getting scolded every single day. He used to dream of a day when he would earn praise from her. It became a mission in his dreary life.

One afternoon, *Memsahib* called him to her cabin. He proceeded with a trembling gait. When he peeped in, she looked up from her busy desk and said: "Good job, Ramchandra! *Aaj sab theekh hua.*" He left the room red-faced. This was the first time in 15 years that anyone had praised him. To receive it from *Memsahib* was the biggest trophy in the world. Just then, Shukla ji walked into the office.

"*Ramchandar, tere bade waale bete ko haiza (cholera) ho gaya hai, doctor ne jawab de diya hai. Tumko jaana hoga.*"

It took Ramchandra a few moments to picture the face of his eldest son. Was he the tall boy who wanted the t-shirt... or the stout one who wanted the shoes? He remembered Chandralekha telling him how the elder one's growth was stunted due to some deficiency. His memory was failing him; he couldn't remember the last time he spoke to his older son.

Just then *Memsahib* stepped out of her cabin and said, "*Shuklaji, Ramchandra bahut accha kaam kar raha hai. Isko idhar hi rakhna ab.*" The two men watched the majestic nymph pass by; her delicate fragrance left a mark on their hearts.

He turned to Shuklaji and said, without stammering, "*Bol do Chandralekha ko, paisa pahuch jaayega...*"

He didn't want to be bothered; he was living his happily ever after.

V

#NoFilter

"C'mon Aashirya, it's time to leave!" As her mother called out, 16-year-old Aashirya struggled to get up from the bed and hobbled towards the door. "Should I look into the mirror before leaving?" she toyed with the thought & turned back to take a peek at her reflection.

As she limped towards the mirror, she remembered how she had fallen in love with this grand dressing table the moment she saw it. It was a huge wooden dresser with large and small drawers that fit everything. The rosewood exterior reflected volumes of luxury. The life-size mirror had bulbs all around it with different settings so that she was able to adjust her make-up according to the time of night or day.

Her mother asked her, "Why do you need such an enormous dresser, Aashirya? You are only 14 years old!" She replied excitedly, "I need it, Maa! I've always wanted one. Don't you remember, I have a similar picture in my scrapbook?" Aashirya preened her hair as she spoke. Her mother yielded and allowed her to have it. The dresser was now her favourite spot in the room. She had organised the drawers with various accessories, make-up material, perfumes, nail polish bottles and other knick-knacks. She spent many hours spritzing perfume, experimenting with make-up & nail polish. When she got the appearance she wanted, she fished out her phone and posed for a selfie. Her favourite Instagram hashtag was #NoFilter.

She had bought a tripod and shot many make-up tutorials on her phone and uploaded them on Instagram. Stories, posts, videos–she did them all. Fashion, lifestyle, beauty were her favourite topics. She spent hours discussing them with her friends on Instagram chats. Every time she posted something on Instagram, she monitored it to check the number of likes, comments, reposts and saves. She rejoiced on the day she crossed 6000 views on her make-up tutorial video. "I will be famous one day, Maa–you just wait and see!" She danced a jig as her mom looked at her.

Ever since the onset of her illness a year and a half ago, the dresser remained the most ignored piece of furniture in her home. They had diagnosed her condition when she was a child. Her father ditched her mom as he couldn't handle the news. Aashirya's mom brought her up single-handedly and kept the devastating news away from her daughter. Just before her 15th birthday, Aashirya had taken to the bed.

Today, she was stepping out of the room for a small *puja* arranged by her mother. Before she reached the mirror, her mom scooped her away. "*Arre*, Maa, it's okay, I want to see. Take me to the mirror, Maa." Her mom supported her and led her to the dresser. Aashirya stepped in front of the mirror & feebly looked at her reflection. A balding scalp with drops of blood oozing from her hives, dry cracked lips and sunken, tired eyes. Tears rolled down her mom's eyes as she looked away. Her lips broke into a half-smile as she picked up a diamond studded comb & attempted to comb her hairless head. She slumped on the seat & adjusted her weak body to face the mirror. With great difficulty, she bent as her bones creaked. With trembling hands, she switched on the lights surrounding the mirror. She felt the harshness of the bulbs & shut them.

Her knees wobbled as she walked into the hall where the *Pandit* was waiting. She sat for some time and then lay on the sofa and slept. After an hour, her mother woke her up and took her back to her room. Aashirya's hands trembled as she opened her scrap book. It contained her bucket list. She smiled as she saw it; she had ticked everything, except one last wish. She continued smiling as she remembered how she had struggled to complete this list. She had no regrets from her life, except one.

"I am sorry Mrs. Rai. Her disease is a rare, congenital one with no proven cure. We tried everything. She has two-three days at max...try to keep her happy, please." For a moment she had regretted eavesdropping on the conversation. But the next moment, she was thankful because she would not leave Mother Earth without ticking off the last item on her bucket list.

She stared at the scrapbook entry for what seemed like forever and then feebly called out, "Maa, maa...! Come here please." Her mom rushed into the room, "What happened? Are you okay, *beta*?" she asked anxiously. "Yes Maa... I am fine. Can you help me get ready? I want to take a picture."

Her mom's eyes were brimming with tears, she was too choked to speak. For the next 25 minutes, she helped Aashirya. Her hands trembled as she applied blush to her daughter's crumbled cheeks. Aashirya requested, "Maa, please can you get my navy-blue shorts and white top?"

Her mom helped her to get dressed. Aashirya had always loved wearing shorts. Her cupboard was full of unique types of shorts, t-shirts and tops. She loved posing as her mom clicked away. Witnessing her daughter struggle to get into her clothes broke the mother's heart. The hives left cruel stains of pus on the clothes–a painful reminder of her disease.

After 45 minutes, Aashirya picked up her mobile phone with trembling hands and clicked a selfie. She adjusted the image and posted it on Instagram with her favourite hashtag, #NoFilter. There was something about her smile - it had a hint of victory in it. As her mom removed her make-up, Aashirya ignored the little mountain of blood-stained cotton swabs on the dresser. She hummed a song and tapped her feet to the beat. Her breathing turned laboured even while she gloated in her own happy world. She turned her head and said, "Watch out Maa, this one will be the best picture with the largest likes & comments. My account will explode with the engagement! My picture will break the internet, Maa." She attempted to laugh, but wheezed and coughed instead. Her mother's heart sank as she gathered her dying baby in her arms.

26 million likes & 4 million comments later, her mom deactivated Aashirya's account and ticked the last item in her daughter's bucket list. She sobbed and prayed that her daughter found peace in heaven. Maybe she had a bucket list in heaven too.

VI
Locked in a closet with a stranger

Jyotsna loved talking on the phone. Her joy knew no bounds when she got a call from her long-lost college friend, Kamya. After an hour of non-stop chattering, she quipped, "I am so happy that we caught up, Kamya, let's meet soon!" Kamya replied, "Same here Jyotsna! Let's meet! You, Ishaan, Kabir, Rudra–our gang! Just like old times."

Jyostna sighed and smiled as she finished the conversation. She made herself a cup of coffee & ambled towards the window. It was a pleasant evening in the busy city of Mumbai. A cool breeze was playing with the trees while birds were returning home and the sun was setting at the horizon. She thanked Mother Nature for the innumerable bounties.

Her schedule was always so busy that she often missed calls from friends. Her husband & kids were out for a swim today. She was feeling bored and therefore, answered Kamya's call. During the conversation, when Kamya mentioned Agastya, her heart gave a twang. She changed the topic. Kamya exclaimed, "The past can hurt. But you can either run from it or learn from it." Jyotsna retorted, "Oh wow! Now you are quoting Lion King! That's a recent development!" They both laughed and continued chatting and exchanging gossip.

She sipped her coffee and laced her fingers around the cup while letting out a sigh. The thoughts of Agastya crossed her mind as she jogged through the memory lane.

Agastya... neither the handsome hunk nor the underdog or the geek. She never noticed him in college. She was the Rose Queen with countless admirers flocking her. He was one of the many faces you see at the Churchgate or CST railway stations. A face that merges into the crowd. She closed her eyes and felt his musty breath on her face. He held her in his muscular arms as they crouched in the closet to save their lives.

Riots broke out in Mumbai on that fateful afternoon. A rumour had ignited the furore: 'a Hindu boy raped his Muslim classmate'. Both communities were angry and had turned irrational. Mumbai was burning even as the police were hunting for the culprit. Jyotsna was in the Physics laboratory at college. When she heard the commotion inside the college, she quickly climbed into the closet. He was already inside.

They had to nestle close in order to fit in. She placed her head on his chest. Her heartbeats were racing at the same pace as his. She let out a long sigh that turned into a slight moan. He shut her mouth with his palms. They smelled of butter. "Hmmn...*pav bhaji*...." She thought to herself.

As a reflex, she avoided eye contact, he nudged her with his nose and whispered, "Everything will be okay... relax..." His grip was reassuring. She mustered courage and looked at him. Had they met earlier? "You have never seen me, but I know who you are..." he replied to the question in her eyes. "You are, Jyotsna, the topper & the most popular girl in First Year Arts! Right?" She struggled for comfort and nodded. He pulled her closer to make more room. His lips touched hers. She moved her face away. His firm grip made her feel secure. She tried to explore what she was feeling, but could fathom nothing. The tension in the air made her stiffen. Agastya gazed at her, smelling her hair as they brushed his cheeks. His fingers danced in pure joy as they held her delicate body. An unknown boy with the famous girl... locked in a closet... wow... a scene straight out of a cheesy novel.

Once again, his lips touched hers and when she moved her face away, he guided it back & kissed her. She was being kissed for the first time in her life. She moved closer & buried her nose in his chest. They were both perspiring and gasping for breath in the tiny closet. They paused for a moment, smiled & continued kissing. There was a loud bang on the closet and the door was flung open. They dragged Agastya out. The furious cop grabbed his hair, kicked him in the groin and screamed the choicest abuses. The policewoman led Jyotsna out of the closet and inquired about her well-being. She was gasping & signalled for water. While gulping the water, she heard the police exclaim,

"*अबबेइतनीखुज़लीथीतोशादीकरलेताखुद्कीबिरादरीमें.*

बलात्कार!!!

वोभीमुसलमानलड़कीका?

अबतोतूगया... बारहकेभावसे!"

(*"If you were in a hurry (to have sex) you should have got married in your community. You have raped a Muslim girl, now you will be doomed forever."*)

She gasped! This guy was the rapist! In those 60 seconds her mind played an infinite number of scenarios of what could have happened. Among the shower of abuses and blows, her eyes caught his. She couldn't believe what she saw in his intense gaze.

A gush of wind brought her back to the present. Life offers a multitude of flavours; she was blessed with the best ones. She sighed & continued her daily routine. She was painting a *mandala*; it helped her focus better. Two hours later, the doorbell rang. As soon as she opened the door, her home was filled with happy squeals. The kids had so many stories to tell their mom. She smiled and listened.

He stepped closer to her and hugged her, "How was your day darling?" She snuggled into his hairy chest as he held her. His firm grip still caused her heart to flutter. She replied, "It was nice. The usual. Have you planned anything special for tomorrow?" He hesitated and said, "I have an important call with the Spain office followed by a meeting with Delhi team. Why?" She shrugged. He was a typical man. He did not remember the anniversary of their first meeting. She replied, "Nothing... just asking. Freshen up, Agastya, I have prepared your favourite meal." He kissed her on the forehead and sauntered into the bedroom, smiling secretly to himself.

Her heart fluttered as she remembered how the police case ended. It was a classic case of mistaken identity for which the police apologised. He was scarred, but she healed him with her love. They got married 6 months after being locked in a closet. Jyostna did not regret a moment since she met him. Never.

VII
Bullet in the heart

My father gave me 3 life rules to live by:
- If you are right, then do not fear anyone
- Walk with your head held high & feet firmly on the ground
- If you have to take sides always side the righteous.

The first 2 were easy, but the third one proved difficult all because of a cheeseburger. Let me explain.

 I grew up in a typical middle-class home in the city of Nagpur where the patriarch ruled the roost. I was blessed to have a family full of happiness and love. Well, to be honest, my father laid the rules, and my mother showered me with unconditional love.

 On my 18th birthday, Papa gifted me a Royal Enfield Bullet 350. The moment I took her by the horns, I knew she was the one for me. Strong & beautiful. When I rode her, the thumping exhaust reminded passers-by of the wonderful time we were having. She was a typical lady - very hard to please. She wouldn't accept a frail, badly groomed man. Only the endowed, well-dressed & fortunate could tame this tigress.

We shared innumerable adventures together. Each moment was a lifetime memory, painted with fun and excitement. She was a one-man woman, or should I say that I didn't allow anyone else to ride her. We romanced our way through my college years, cruised through MBA and zipped into work life.

This continued until Bindiya entered my life... she was just like her name, dainty, like a 'dewdrop'. Her million-dollar smile lit up the conference room at work. She was the life of every party and engulfed everyone in the room with her positivity and warmth. Everyone at the office was always praising her no-nonsense attitude, commitment to work & intelligence. She worked in the accounts audit department and was famous for her numerical prowess.

The office's *chai-tapri* gang secretly praised her 'assets' & wondered if she would allow them to 'tally'. Bindiya had an innovative way of keeping her distance from unwanted liabilities. Every once in a while, she scouted for a companion & hooked up with somebody at work or outside. She flaunted him in a manner that other men stayed far away from her. This time around, she chose me among the eligible bachelors at the office.

We were now the power of three; my Bullet, Bindiya, and me. We took off on lengthy rides, racing against the breeze. Only the boys know what it means to ride a Bullet with a hot, sexy woman on the pillion seat. I was the object of envy at work. I gloated with pride as we whizzed past the *chai-tapri* gang.

I had the best of both worlds. I just could not decide what was better, mounting Bindiya or my Bullet. Both gave me the ultimate feeling of masculinity. I ensured that I divided my time between the 2 ladies. The balancing act was tough but manageable. Everything was going great until that fateful day.

It was Christmas eve, and celebrating it in a grand manner was the latest fad. A decorated tree adorned the office lobby with little piles of gifts all around it. The typical 'Jingle-bells' song was played all day–it irritated me to the core! No one knew what Christmas meant. They were all celebrating 'Secret Santa' and the girls squealed in excitement each time someone's name was called out. It was so irritating! I wanted to leave and signalled Bindiya again and again. She was dancing and insisted on staying and taking part in the jamboree. I stormed out of the party with Bindiya in tow. We stopped at my Bullet.

Her gait was unsteady, and she slipped many times while following me. "Rohit, what is wrong with you, it's Christmas!! Let's enjoy the party!" Her speech was slurred. How can a woman let down her guard this way? I put my arm around her and said, "Stop it Bindiya, let me drop you home, you have had too much to drink." She pushed me away and waved a cheeseburger in the air and muttered something. The cheese was oozing out of the burger, making a mess. She moved away as she waved the burger, "Nonsense, I am just fff...ii...nee! Have a bite of this cheeseburger, it's yuuummmyyyyyy....mmmmmeeeee!" She giggled and rolled her eyes. My annoyance was at its peak, I flicked her hand aside. Colossal mistake! The cheeseburger flew out of her hand and landed on my Bullet. The cheese trickled out of the bun and stained the seat. I gaped in utter horror! The scene before me was horrid! My favourite woman was in trouble.

Bindiya looked at my expression and came back to her senses. She started apologising, "Oh gosh.... Sssorry.... Rohit... ohhh... I... I... I am.... I am... so sorry, Rohit! Sooooo sorryyyyy..."

She fished out a tissue and started rubbing the seat. Since her hands were not steady, she spread it even more. The Bullet was now decorated with cheese, mustard, mayonnaise, and pickles. The bun rolled down and got stuck in the spokes. I was seething with anger. I growled and wielded a tight slap on Bindiya's cute face. "How dare you, you bitch! How dare you touch my baby!" Her cheeks turned red as my fingers got imprinted on them. She screamed in agony, turned, and hit me back. What followed was a scuffle, a struggle for power. Or was it her exasperation for losing the race to the Bullet?

She kicked me in the stomach, I charged towards her. When I pulled her hair, she screamed and struggled to get loose. She stepped back and landed on the Bullet. I did not notice and pushed her hard. The Bullet got dislodged and fell to the ground. Oh gosh! Both my ladies were on the ground! Which one should I pick up first? I picked up the Bullet and put her back on the stand. I then proceeded to pick up Bindiya. Shock, pain, and anger were written all over her face. She was bleeding. I took her inside and left her with my colleagues who rushed to our rescue. I ran out to take care of my baby.

My heart skipped a beat as I saw her standing in the parking lot as if nothing had happened. She never complained or nagged me. It was as if she understood me and had put this incident behind her. Why can't other women be like her? That was the last day I dated Bindiya. It was difficult to follow what Papa taught me but I had to take sides, I chose to stay with the righteous. A mere girl could not come in between me and the love of my life.

Six months later, I attended Bindiya's wedding. She married Shankar from the *chai-tapri* gang. He hated motorbikes and detested all two-wheelers. I looked at him as he smugly smiled at me from the stage. Urrghh... he hates bikes? Is he even a man? Bindiya greeted me with her signature smile. She looked splendid that day. Her captivating smile made me go stiff, but melting was not a choice.

That evening I rode my Bullet at 120 Kmph with a bullet in my heart.

VIII
The Devil's Bride

The whirring noise of the fan & the creak of the unbolted door woke her. Her throat was parched. She licked her moist lips and realised that her own blood was quenching her thirst. She wiped her mouth with the back of her dirty, bruised hand. Her head was throbbing right where he had pulled her hair while dragging her from the bedroom to the hall.

She lay there for a moment; it served as a respite from his torturous behaviour. Each time he returned from his weekly tours, he lashed out his frustration on her. The neighbours often heard his growls and her cries for help. They ignored the sound of whiplashes followed by pain-filled moans and loud crying. Her neighbours and friends urged her to walk out of her marriage. But, none of them had the guts to stand up in front of this monster to protect her. She knew that these 'well-wishers' will not house her if she ever leaves him.

During the initial days, she used to sob over the phone to her mother. When her parents came to talk to him, he threatened them with a knife and threw them out of the house. After that day, her parents left her to fate.

She shuddered in fright on the days he came with his shirt tucked out. It was an indication that the night was going to be a difficult one. He sat on the sofa with his ugly belly popping out of his vest. On his cue, she entered the room with a tray of drinks and food in her hand. She paraded stark naked through the room; her eyes filled with tears of shame. He played sleazy music on the home theatre and asked her to dance to the beats. She had to jiggle her breasts and hips to titillate his senses. He passed lewd remarks as she walked in with the tray. Like a ravenous animal he slapped her bottom and tugged at her breasts. After forcing her to do weird sexual acts, he threw money on her face and hurled abuses at her.

On other nights, after guzzling half a bottle, he pinned her on the floor and forced himself on her. She suffocated under his weight and when she cringed in pain, he slapped her and asked her to smile. She smiled through her tears as he tried to get his job done. He tried to get a hard-on and kept thrusting into her. The empty thumps filled the room as she moaned. He growled, "*Mazza aa raha hai? Bol, mazza aa raha hai?*" She nodded through her tears, but he was unable to get a boner. He pushed her aside and his fists rained on her naked body like burning hailstones.

Whenever he was tired of beating her, he withdrew into the bedroom, grunting. After he slept, she gathered herself, put on clothes and went to sleep beside him. She hugged him and slept; he hugged her back. She felt safe with him–this was her fate, her only fate.

The next morning, he behaved as if nothing had happened. He hugged her and kissed her on the forehead before leaving for work. She smiled back and handed him his lunch. After he left, she sobbed miserably as she nursed her bruises.

Where could she go? Live alone? That was easier said than done. He took care of every material comfort. They were better off compared to her siblings, parents or friends. Her parents had married her off even before she completed her graduation. No employer would give her a job with a salary that could match her current lifestyle.

Night after night, he found different ways of torturing her while attempting sex. He sometimes tried unnatural ways of getting pleasure. She bore it, and when he failed, he beat her black and blue. Sometimes, he buried his head in her chest and cried himself to sleep. On other days, she lay her aching head on his broad shoulders and slept like a disturbed baby.

She came back to reality, and her eyes searched him. It was late at night and almost time for the customary cuddle after the beating. Her bosom missed his sweaty face and stinking breath. Where was he today? Why was he so silent? The sound of sirens pierced through the air. She adjusted her torn clothes that revealed old & new gashes, some oozing blood and others, oozing pus. The clothes were torn in a way that half a breast & shoulder was exposed. She gathered all her strength and hobbled towards the window, wondering what the commotion was about. She looked out of the window and gasped in horror. Was that him...? ... How... who... when...?

She closed her eyes like a frightened kitten. She was greeted by flashes of her rising like a tigress. A mighty tigress who had pawed his ugly face, ferociously bit his neck, picked him up and hurled him down from their penthouse. A weak smile appeared on her tired, blood-stained face. She heaved a sigh of relief as she plonked herself on the sofa and passed out. When she opened her eyes at the hospital, she learned that a case of accidental death was registered to his name. She stared at the nurse as she narrated the police findings. After the nurse left, she closed her eyes and whispered a prayer.

The office arranged for the insurance compensation. Her hands did not tremble as she received the 10-crore cheque. She adjusted her dress, smiled slightly, bowed her head and walked away. There was an unconventional spring in her step today.

The tigress, will now rule... forever.

IX

A God named Sin

She often wondered if she was the only one who felt lonely in a crowd. Her eyes were always searching for Suraj. Her nose hunted for his steel breath all the time. Whenever her husband, Akash touched her, she tried to imagine Suraj's soft touch. Every evening, Akash hugged her tightly, and she rested her tired head on his shoulder. He ran his fingers slowly across her back as she was unwinding; she yearned for Suraj's tickles. She shut her eyes tightly each time Akash made love to her. Just when they were about to climax, she secretly opened her eyes. She could not find what she was looking for. Disappointed, she faked an orgasm and pretended to sleep.

Akash and his family had no reason to complain about Reena. She was coy, dutiful and obedient. She took care of everyone's needs and was always smiling. Akash often nudged her and asked her if anything was bothering her. He always wondered what lay behind her stoic & mysterious silence. She replied sweetly, "Nothing. Nothing at all. I am like this only. I have always been quiet." Her mind drifted to carefree childhood days when she was famous for her pranks. Complaints from neighbours, teachers, and peers were common. Her loud laughter echoed through the narrow lanes of her colony. Over the years, she had left the playful Reena far behind.

Today, her life was perfect. Akash doted on her. She was the ideal wife who had gifted him two angelic children. Her in-laws adored her and he was very respectful and loving towards her parents. She had her space, and he had his. But something was missing.

One day, she was leafing through an old diary when she found a crumpled piece of paper. She opened it. Some written portions were blotted, maybe because of tears. Her face fell as she started reading.

Unspoken words

There is a lot to tell and much to express,
A loss of words and an urge to impress,
Nothing can reflect my hesitation,
Now that I've faced rejection,
My wounds are eternal and will never heal,
The unspoken words won't tell what I feel!

Tears rolled down her cheeks as she put the paper away. Her mind was flooded with how Suraj had uncermoniously broken up with her. It was her 17th birthday, and he had not been responding to her texts for over a fortnight. She gathered courage and dialled his landline. His mom answered and told Reena that Suraj did not want to have anything to do with her. She spent her birthday feigning happiness as her friends and family showered gifts and blessings on her. She sobbed into her pillow at night and asked God repeatedly, "How could he do this to me? How could he ditch me like this? He had promised to be with me till eternity."

Her phone's beep brought her back to reality. It was a friend request on Facebook. The tears disappeared, and a warm glow lit up her face. She was blushing after so long. It was Suraj! She was about to accept the request when she stopped herself. What if Akash came to know? She had stalked Suraj's social media profile almost every day. He was married and had two growing boys. He seemed happy by the look of the social media pictures. She often wondered if he missed her.

She could never forget the day she lost her virginity. She remembered the first time they were alone at his home. One thing had led to another, and they had made love. They were both inexperienced, and it was this that made the experience the best ever to date. He was 20 years old, and she was about to turn 17 in a week. They forgot about a condom and made crazy love several times that afternoon. Their bodies were intertwined as they lay naked on Suraj's parents' bed. They were so lost in love that they did not realise that his parents had the keys to the home. They were startled and embarrassed when his mother opened the bedroom door and found them on her bed. Reena dressed up and ran out of the house. It was after this incident that Suraj had abruptly broken off their affair. She never forgot his touch. Her prayers were answered when she received the friend request from him. Despite the passage of time, their love was still intact.

After a week of hesitation, she accepted the request at 7 AM one sunny morning. As soon as she did so, a message popped up, "Hey"–she was taken aback. It was as if he was waiting. She typed, "Hi". He went offline at once. She sighed and returned to cooking for her family. After about 2 hours, her phone pinged once again. "Sorry, the time difference creates havoc. I dozed off in the middle of our chat.

Apologies." She smiled as she read each word twice. "Time difference?" she asked. "Yes, I stay in Dubai and so it's about 6:30 AM here" he replied. "*Bahu! Aajao, chai peete hai saath mein!*" It was her mother-in-law calling her for their morning *chai* routine. She shut the phone and entered the dining room. Her mother-in-law was her usual chatty self, and she narrated interesting gossip to her patient daughter-in-law.

Throughout the day, she kept thinking about him. Her phone kept beeping even as she was completing her housework. When the beeping didn't stop, she smuggled the phone into the bathroom and read his texts. She replied, and he replied back. This became a routine and over the next few days, they chatted regularly.

She rejoiced when she realised that Akash's tour to Germany coincided with Suraj's travel to India. She sought permission from her husband and in-laws to attend a 'meditation camp' in a remote location,120 kms away from the city. They agreed because this was the first time, she was doing something for herself. She spent an entire day at the salon to get ready for the meeting. She bore excruciating pain and underwent the bikini wax. She armed herself with the I-pill and a pack of condoms.

They met in the hotel lobby, "You look even more beautiful now, Reena." He exclaimed in awe. "You have changed a lot, Suraj. You haven't been taking care of yourself, have you?" was referring to his receding hairline and slight paunch. He chuckled as they proceeded to the room. He hugged her the moment the door closed behind them. She found the same sensation - finally!

But it felt different. She looked at him as he pecked her on the cheek. She moved away and sat on the sofa. He bent towards her; it was the same steel breath, but this time it was mixed in nicotine. He put his face close to hers and whispered, "*Jaan*... it's me...!" He kissed her and in no time their clothes slipped off from their bodies, her naked body touched his.

Instead of feeling good, she winced. This was wrong. Akash did not deserve this. She started dressing up when Suraj pulled her back and kissed her once again. She moaned slightly as he rubbed his tool on her front parts. She continued to moan. They made deep, intense, and passionate love. She climaxed numerous times that afternoon. When he was riding her, she opened her eyes and shut them happily when she realised it was her own Suraj. They made love countless times over the next 3 days.

These sessions were interspersed by giggling about days of yore. They bathed together, ate together, and lived the dream life that they always wanted to. On the third day, in between a mind-blowing love-making session, he asked her, "Do you still love me, Reena?" She stopped moaning and looked into his eyes quizzically. She signalled him to continue thrusting his manliness into her hungry being. She turned her head and shut her eyes tightly. The truth dawned.

He fell asleep soon after they finished. She dressed up and gathered all her clothes and tip-toed out of the room. She left a note beside his table and left for her home. On her way back, she blocked Suraj's profile on all her social media platforms. She spent hours in the family temple praying and asking forgiveness for her sins. A week later, when Akash returned, she hugged him tightly.

A perplexed Suraj returned to his loveless life and empty home. In his pocket was a note that said, "Thank you, God of Sin. Bye, forever."

Author Bio

Mayura Amarkant is an entrepreneur, blogger, promoter of a theatre group, and a prominent writer.

In 2017, Mayura was conferred a national-level award, as a Woman Business Leader in Digital Marketing and Public Relations by the Indo-Global SME Chamber.

Her agency, Sarvashreshtha Solutions, specializes in digital and online innovations. She is a psychology graduate and a postgraduate in Human Resources & has a

AUTHOR BIO

Master's in Neurolinguistic Programming.

Mayura is a doctoral student with a research interest in Women & Leadership. Her blog, DiaryOfAnInsaneWriter, is among the top lifestyle blogs in India and attracts visitors from over 125 countries. She is a proponent of live art and promotes talent through the Karwan Theatre Group. Armed with over 2 decades of experience, Mayura has written education-related cover features for top newspapers. She has compiled study material, edited coffee-table books, novels, brochures, and articles.

Her scripts have given form to many corporate movies. She has also curated content for a web series. Even today, she continues to ghost-write for many corporates. She is a fitness freak and an award-winning sportsperson who plays cricket, throw ball, and runs marathons.

Trapped in Heaven is Mayura's first anthology of romance fiction. With this book, she has also launched Sansi Ventures, the publishing arm of Sarvashreshtha Solutions.

You can reach Mayura on: diaryofaninsanewriter@gmail.com.

www.ingramcontent.com/pod-product-compliance
Lightning Source LLC
LaVergne TN
LVHW042002060526
838200LV00041B/1827